The Smallest Girl Ever

Sally Gardner is the author and illustrator of *The Fairy
Catalogue*, *A Book of Princesses* and other popular books
for children. She started out as a designer of sets and
costumes for the theatre. She has a son and twin daughters
and lives in London.

The Smallest Girl Ever

Sally Gardner

Dolphin

First published in Great Britain in 2000
by Dolphin Paperbacks
Reissued 2002 by Dolphin Paperbacks
an imprint of Orion Children's Books
a division of the Orion Publishing Group Ltd
Orion House
5 Upper St Martin's Lane
London WC2H 9EA

10

Text and illustrations copyright © Sally Gardner 2000

The moral rights of the author have been asserted.

The Orion Publishing Group's policy is to use papers that
are natural, renewable and recyclable products and
made from wood grown in sustainable forests. The logging
and manufacturing processes are expected to conform to
the environmental regulations of the country of origin.

A catalogue record for this book is available
from the British Library

Printed in Great Britain by
Clays Ltd, St Ives plc

ISBN-13 978 1 85881 707 1

www.orionbooks.co.uk

To a life sadly ended: Joan Gardner

And a life just begun: Ruby O'Kane

1

Mr and Mrs Genie wanted a baby.

They had always got what they wanted, so they were sure they would have a son. He would grow up to be a great genie like his father and a great magician like his mother. Mr Genie was the latest in a long line of genies dating back to the earliest fairy tales, and his beautiful wife Myrtle won the Young Magician of the Year competition when she was only five. Magic ran in the family.

There was only one snag. Mr and Mrs Genie had a little girl.

"A girl!" wailed Myrtle. "I wanted a son and heir! There must be some terrible mistake."

"This is too much!" said Mr Genie. "Never in all my life have I failed to make a wish come true!"

Myrtle sobbed miserably.

"Never mind, my darling," said Mr Genie, trying to be cheerful. "We can always have a boy next time."

Mr and Mrs Genie did their best to get over the shock. It was very hard. They started making plans. They finally called the baby Ruby, and put her name down for Wizodean Academy. This was one of the world's top schools for magic, and prided itself on only taking exceptional boys and girls.

But by the time Ruby was six, she had shown no sign of any early magical talent.

Neither did she have a baby brother.

"Where did we go wrong?" cried Myrtle. "We still haven't got the son we wanted and planned for. All we have is a daughter with no magical talent. It hardly seems worth all the effort and inconvenience of having a baby."

Things might have gone better if Ruby had been a great beauty like her mother. Sad to say, she was a rather a plain-looking girl. In short, Ruby was a huge disappointment.

Mr Genie and Mrs Genie were far too big stars to be bothered with a child who showed no magical talent. They were at the height of their fame. They threw huge parties, featured in all the papers, wore expensive clothes, owned the Ferrari of flying carpets and never gave money a thought. Why should they? They were, after all, entertaining the rich and famous and were in huge demand all over the world.

So Ruby stayed at home with a dull but kind nanny, kept well away from the razzamatazz that made up her parents' life.

Nanny didn't believe in magic. She believed in the three Rs: reading, routine and rules. This way Ruby Genie, more forgotten by her parents than thought about, managed to reach the grand age of nine without once having gone to school. Ruby would have liked to go to the local school with the other boys and girls of her own age, but this was out of the question. Since she had failed to pass the entrance exam for Wizodean Academy, her parents had lost all interest in her education. Which was a pity, for Nanny had taught her to read well and she was quick to learn.

But reading and writing meant nothing to Mr and Mrs Genie. A child who could do magic shouldn't need to bother with all that. Ruby might be able to read Cinderella, but it would be far better if she could turn pumpkins into carriages.

"You'll just have to work harder at your magic," said her mother.

"I'm sure you're just not concentrating enough on your spells," said her father.

"Oh dear," said Nanny. "No good will come of all this magical nonsense."

And Nanny was right.

2

Just before Ruby's tenth birthday, the
emperor of Tishshan, a small and much
overlooked state on the borders of China,
invited Mr and Mrs Genie to perform a
magical feat that hadn't been attempted
since the pyramids were built. This was far
too tempting a challenge. Sad to say, it also
proved to be the death of Mr and Mrs
Genie, who disappeared in a spectacular
meteor of fireworks. All that was left

behind was a lamp, a wand and a pile of unpaid bills.

To lose one parent is a terrible misfortune. To lose two is just plain silly, and tends to turn the future upside down. At the tender age of ten, Ruby was an orphan.

The bad news brought with it a lawyer, who appeared like a rabbit pulled from a top hat.

"A very sad business. Such great stars! I remember seeing them perform live at the Met in New York. Quite wonderful! Unfortunately, not so wonderful with money. In short, and not to put too fine a point on it, the house will have to be sold."

"But what about Ruby?" interrupted Nanny. "What's going to happen to her?"

"Ruby," said the lawyer, searching his papers. "It says nothing about jewellery. Any jewellery will of course have to be sold."

"No, no!" said Nanny crossly. "Their little girl, Ruby."

The lawyer looked quite surprised to find there was a little girl in the room. He pulled even more papers out of his briefcase.

"Here I have it." He cleared his throat and read, "In case of any unforeseen misfortune like death, having no other living relatives, Ruby, the only child of the late Mr and Mrs Genie, is to go to a boarding school for magic."

"But that's ridiculous!" said Nanny. "The girl can't do any magic."

"That," said the lawyer, "is not my problem."

Finding a school of magic that would take Ruby was difficult. She tried once more to get into Wizodean Academy. Not surprisingly, she failed. The school refused to take a child with no magical talent, even if she was the daughter of Mr and Mrs Genie, and they felt it was a great mistake that she had been allowed to learn reading and writing.

Ruby also failed to get a place at several other well-known schools for magic, for the same reasons.

"If only they had wanted you to go to a normal school instead of all this magical nonsense," said Nanny, as yet another refusal letter landed on the doormat.

The house was being packed up around Ruby and still no school had been found. The lawyer was becoming concerned.

"There are always orphanages," he said gravely.

Then out of the blue, just before the removal van arrived, came a letter from Grimlocks School for Conjurers and Magicians. To everyone's amazement Ruby was being offered a scholarship. The lawyer accepted the place immediately without putting himself through the inconvenience of looking at the school.

No time was wasted in packing Ruby up. All she owned in the world went into her suitcase: her new school uniform, her mum's wand and her dad's lamp. These she had been given by the lawyer, who thought, wrongly, that they had little value except to Ruby.

Nanny said a tearful goodbye. She was sad to be leaving Ruby, but delighted to be taking a job with no magic in it whatsoever. She was going to look after a little baby boy whose parents were librarians.

"Look after yourself, and remember the

three Rs," she said. A Sold sign went up outside Ruby's house. The lawyer snapped shut his briefcase, shook Ruby's hand and was gone, as was everything else that had made up Ruby's life.

3

"Grimlocks School? Never heard of it," said the taxi driver. Ruby showed him the address again. They had been driving around in circles. Ruby was sure they were completely lost when they came across a battered sign covered with ivy.

As they drove up the drive, Ruby's heart began to sink. The mock Tudor building, half hidden in a dark wood, was a gloomy sight.

"Not a very cheerful-looking place," said the taxi driver, helping Ruby out with her suitcase. "Are you sure you're going to be all right?"

At that moment the front door opened and the headmistress, Miss Pinkerton, came out. She was a large lady shaped like a bell.

"Ruby Genie? We have been waiting for you," she said briskly. "This way, if you please."

"Good luck," said the taxi driver.

Ruby was shown into the headmistress's office. The room was full of noisy ticking clocks of various shapes and sizes.

"A little hobby of mine," said Miss Pinkerton. "Well, sit down."

Ruby sat, or rather perched, on the edge of a huge chair.

"I must say how pleased we are to welcome you to Grimlocks. We are not a big school, but our aim is to turn out boys and girls who are a credit to the world of magic. You are the first child ever to be given a scholarship by us. We feel sure that with such brilliant parents you are bound to be a very gifted little girl. Now, I will tell you what we expect from our star student."

Ruby was never to find out what was expected of her for, at that moment, all the clocks started to chime one after another. It was a whole five minutes before she could hear one word of what the headmistress was saying. Then Miss Pinkerton stood up.

"Glad we sorted all that out," she said.

Ruby felt the moment had passed to say anything about not having any magical talent. Miss Pinkerton did not move. She kept looking at Ruby as if waiting for something.

"Haven't you got something for me, Ruby?" she said at last.

Ruby looked baffled.

"The lamp, your father's lamp!" said Miss Pinkerton. Ruby opened up her small suitcase and took out the lamp. The headmistress seized it and held it up to her ample bosom.

"To hold such a lamp as this!" she cried

in tones of delight, before locking it up in a glass display case.

"But I would rather like to keep it with me, if it's all the same to you," said Ruby. "It's all I've got to remember my father by."

This was not the right thing to say. Miss Pinkerton seemed to puff herself up like a toad.

"Keep it!" she said, going very red in the face. "A lamp of this magnitude in the hands of a child! You must be out of your mind. Did I see a wand in your suitcase, too? Give it to me, please."

The wand was put in her desk along with peashooters, stink bombs, catapults and all the other things the children were not allowed.

After Ruby had unpacked, she was taken into the dining hall. A smell of stale cabbage greeted her. About fifty children were seated on benches at two long wooden tables.

"This is our scholarship pupil, Ruby Genie," said Miss Pinkerton.

Ruby took her place at the table between a boy called Zack and a girl called Lily whose hair was in plaits.

"You couldn't turn this into chips and sausages with lots of tomato sauce, could you?" said Zack hopefully.

"No," said Ruby sadly, looking down at the pale grey lumpy things that made up supper.

"It must be wonderful to be as good at magic as you," Lily said.

Ruby smiled weakly. She wished more than anything that she was.

4

The next day, in the school assembly, Miss Pinkerton was in a good mood. It had been a stroke of brilliance, she thought, to offer Ruby a scholarship. It couldn't be a better advertisement for Grimlocks and was bound to bring in other children whose parents had money that was much needed. It would also keep the Grand Wizard happy. Last year, he had nearly closed the school down due to its bad teaching and dilapidated buildings.

"Now, children," said Miss Pinkerton, giving a rare and terrible smile. "You have by now all met our star pupil, Ruby. Ruby dear, will you come up here."

Ruby walked up on to the stage at the end of the hall where the staff and headmistress were seated.

"I'd like to introduce you to our staff. Miss Fisher, magimatics; Mr Gaspard, conjuring tricks; Madame Vanish, grand illusions; and lastly myself, special effects. Now Ruby, I am sure you can't wait to show us your magical skills so I thought you could start by doing something simple, like a little flying or perhaps a disappearing act."

Ruby felt her knees begin to shake. She stood in front of the whole school, hoping that the floor would open and swallow her up. There was a moment of dreadful silence as she stood frozen to the spot. Everyone was looking at her.

"When you are ready," said Miss Pinkerton impatiently.

Ruby felt herself getting smaller, a very strange sensation. Suddenly she had a brainwave.

"I'm awfully sorry but I only ever did magic with my mum and dad. I'm not used to having so many people watching."

Miss Pinkerton looked much relieved at this explanation and said in a very solemn voice to the whole school, "Ruby has suffered the dreadful loss of her parents, the great Mr Genie and his wife Myrtle. We must give her time to settle down, but I'm sure in due course Ruby will amaze us with her magical ability and no doubt be able to teach all of us a thing or two."

Ruby wasn't sure about that. All she knew was that she felt smaller.

"That's pretty cool," said Zack.

"What is?" said Ruby nervously.

"The way you shrank just now."

5

If this was what school was about, it must
all be a dreadful mistake. How could any
kind or loving parent send their child here?
As far as Ruby could see, all the parents who
had children at the school thought they
were doing the very best for them. Zack's
mum worked overtime in the circus so that
she could pay the school fees. Lily's dad and
mum hadn't been on holiday for years so
they could afford to send her to Grimlocks.

This seemed true for most of the pupils.

It soon became clear to Ruby that none of the teachers knew all that much about magic. She remembered her father saying in an interview for a Sunday paper that magic couldn't be taught. It came from the heart. You either had it or you didn't. Ruby knew she didn't.

Ruby couldn't make head or tail of the lessons in magic. Madame Vanish's classes seemed to be in another language altogether. Ruby could hardly understand one word of what she was saying, so there was no hope of her learning anything about illusions. Miss Pinkerton's classes were the dullest, and went on for ever. They had little or nothing to do with special effects, but a great deal to do with money, or rather the lack of it. Miss Pinkerton constantly reminded them how expensive it was to run a school like Grimlocks and how she needed to raise more money for a spells lab.

Mr Gaspard's conjuring classes were the best. Everyone enjoyed them. In his youth he had starred at the Lyceum Theatre, but it burnt down in mysterious circumstances. What these were he wouldn't say, but a lot of his conjuring involved smoke and most of his lessons ended in a loud bang. He was kind to Ruby and seemed to understand that she was doing her best.

What saved Ruby and made her more friends than any amount of magic was reading. No other child in the school could read. Reading, writing and arithmetic were not on the school curriculum. The theory was that truly magical children didn't need to be taught these harmful subjects. Reading gave children the wrong ideas.

Ruby's success lay in her old fairy tale book, which she read to her friends after lights out at night. All her friends agreed that reading was quite an amazing magic trick and they all wanted to be able to do it.

Mr Gaspard would let Ruby off having to do any magic, as long as she read aloud to the class. So Ruby managed to get out of having to do anything spectacular - but it couldn't last. Miss Fisher, who taught magimatics, did not like it one little bit when she found that Ruby could read, and she told Miss Pinkerton so.

"What we need," said Miss Fisher, "is a scholarship student who excels in magimatics, not reading."

Miss Pinkerton agreed. "Her father, you know, was an exceptionally clever genie. Perhaps he felt it was all right for her to read."

Miss Fisher sniffed. "So far she has shown no ability at all in the field of magic."

"I'm sure," said Miss Pinkerton, "that when she has settled down, we will find that we made an excellent choice in giving her a scholarship."

"Well, I hope you're right, Headmistress, because I don't think it will go down at all well with the Grand Wizard if he finds out that we have given our one and only scholarship to a dud."

6

It was the time of year when the Grand
Wizard made his annual visit, and Miss
Pinkerton was in a panic. She knew he
would not hesitate to close the school down
if things hadn't improved.

On the whole, there was very little
magic attached to getting the school ready
for inspection. It was more like a lot of hard
work. It was generally agreed that rain
would be a bad idea, so a shabby old

marquee was put up in the grounds and
Madame Vanish did a magic spell to keep
the rain away (well, that was what
everyone thought she was doing).

Mr Gaspard was hard at work in the
kitchen, trying to conjure up a magnificent
tea. Lily was helping him. After a lot of
explosions with flour, Miss Pinkerton said it
would be better to order some cakes from
the bakery.

As for Ruby, she was sitting alone in an
empty classroom, wondering what she was

going to do. Miss Pinkerton had given her a list of tricks she was expected to perform for the Grand Wizard, and she was excused from all the classes so she could practise. But it was no good. She still hadn't done one thing to merit a place, let alone a scholarship, at Grimlocks.

Her friends Lily and Zack tried their best to help her. Lily wondered if she could make a smokescreen to distract the Grand Wizard, since she was one of Mr Gaspard's star pupils. Zack felt the best thing she could do would be to disappear for the day, but this didn't look possible, not with Miss Pinkerton's beady eye on her.

In the end, Lily said, "You could try reading him a story. Perhaps he can't read either."

7

Finally the day of the visit arrived, and it rained. The children were all neatly turned out and if you half shut your eyes, the school looked passable. Miss Pinkerton had made a great show the night before of making the final special effect. Everyone had clapped though no difference could be seen whatsoever.

The Grand Wizard was a tall man with a long beard that trailed on the floor. He didn't seem much impressed with anything Grimlocks School had to offer. He watched despairingly as one of the juniors did a piece of magic involving fire and smoke that nearly resulted in setting the marquee alight. He sat, grim-faced, as a senior did a mysterious disappearing act and failed to reappear. Tea did not make things any better. The sandwiches were soggy from the rain and the water that had been used to put out the fire. And for some reason, the cook had gone missing as had all the cakes that Miss Pinkerton had ordered at vast expense from the local bakery.

In short, the Grand Wizard was not in a good mood.

"We have of course our scholarship student," said Miss Pinkerton desperately. "I'm sure, Grand Wizard, you would like to see some of her truly amazing magic."

"It would make a change, Miss Pinkerton, to see anything magical at this school," replied the Grand Wizard.

"Ruby, come here, my dear," called Miss Pinkerton. "Grand Wizard, this is Ruby. Her parents . . ."

"Yes, yes," said the Grand Wizard. "Do you think that we could get to the magic? I do have a dinner appointment at Wizodean Academy that I would like to keep."

This was the moment that Ruby had been dreading. She had been practising a little magic show which involved pulling a rabbit from a hat, followed by two doves. The rabbit and doves were under the table in two separate baskets. The trouble was she hadn't mastered how to get the rabbit and the doves from the baskets into the hat. She could do it if no one was looking. But everybody was looking and Miss Pinkerton, in particular, was looking furious. Mr Gaspard was looking worried, Madame Vanish was looking bored and Miss Fisher, on the other hand, was looking smug.

At that moment, Ruby knocked over the baskets. The rabbit hopped out from under the table and started nibbling the Grand Wizard's beard and the doves flew away into the rafters.

Once again, Ruby felt herself shrinking with fear, getting smaller by the second. Nothing for it but to tell the truth, she thought.

"I can't do magic! It's all been a terrible mistake. I can read, and I can write, but I can't do magic. My parents could, but I can't." At that moment, a dove's poo plopped on to the Grand Wizard's shoulder.

The Grand Wizard stared hard at Ruby and turned pale.

"What is the name of this girl?" he asked, pointing at her.

"Ruby Genie," said Miss Pinkerton apologetically. "Don't worry, Grand Wizard, she's in good hands."

8

It had gone worse than even Ruby thought possible. The Grand Wizard had stared at her for a long time and then left without saying a word. Miss Pinkerton frogmarched Ruby into her office.

"How, I would like to know, did two such brilliant magicians manage to have such a stupid daughter?" shouted Miss Pinkerton, going purple with rage.

"You have let me down, young lady,

and the whole of the school as well," she yelled above the deafening noise of the chiming clocks. "I would like you to leave immediately but unfortunately I find, much to my annoyance, that there is nowhere to send you. So, for the time being, you will have to stay here and help in the kitchen."

"It's not as bad as all that," said Lily later, trying to sound cheerful.

"How do you make that out?" said Ruby gloomily. "I'm no good at magic. I have just upset the Grand Wizard. The school is most probably going to be shut down. I have to work in the kitchen, and to make matters worse, I won't ever get my lamp or wand back."

"If the school shuts down you can come home with me," said Lily brightly. "Mum and Dad would know what to do. I'm sure they could help."

"Thanks," said Ruby.

"I'm sure something will turn up," said Lily, trying to sound encouraging.

9

What turned up was as much a surprise to Ruby as it was to Miss Pinkerton. It seemed that Ruby had an uncle.

Ruby's uncle was a large, jolly man who looked like an actor in need of a theatre.

"I have searched the four corners of the globe to find my little niece, and here she is, hidden away in your excellent school," he boomed to Miss Pinkerton. "Allow me to introduce myself. I am the Great Alfonso, brother of the late Mr Genie, and devoted uncle of Ruby Genie." He looked a little taken aback by the sight of Ruby.

"Are you telling me, Miss Pinkerton, that this wee girl is ten? She looks more like six to my untrained eye. What have you done to her? Starved her?"

Miss Pinkerton looked flustered. "No, no such thing. Ruby has just got smaller, all of her own accord. Nothing, I can assure you, to do with us. No, nothing at all."

"Oh my poor little niece," said Alfonso. "Tell me, what have they done to you?"

Ruby wasn't sure what to say. Miss Pinkerton was glaring at her.

"Never mind," said Alfonso. "Put it all behind you. We have the future in front of us." He paused, then said, "The lamp, where is the lamp?"

Miss Pinkerton looked quite put out.

"I feel that as Ruby has caused us so much trouble and expense, the lamp is a small price to pay for her school fees."

Alfonso's face clouded over. "You toy with me, the Great Alfonso, at your peril," he said. "My brother's lamp in exchange for a stay at your school! Madam, have you completely lost your marbles? That lamp is priceless," he said, putting an arm round Ruby. "Priceless to us, his only remaining family."

Miss Pinkerton looked suddenly defeated and handed over the lamp. As Alfonso took it from her, the frown lifted from his face. He waved his arms and the lamp vanished into his coat. Ruby looked on amazed.

"My mother's wand," she whispered to Alfonso. Miss Pinkerton realized she had met her match. She went over to her desk and handed the wand to Alfonso. In the twinkling of an eye, the wand vanished too.

"How do you do that?" said Ruby, really impressed.

"Later, my dear child, later." He turned and bowed to Miss Pinkerton. "I hope, dear lady," he said, taking her hand and kissing it, "that with a little extra tuition Ruby will soon be taking up her place again at Grimlocks."

Miss Pinkerton looked doubtful and was about to say so when she was rudely interrupted by all the clocks striking twelve.

10

"Is that your tummy rumbling or distant thunder?" said Alfonso merrily as they were driving away from Grimlocks.

"It's my tummy," said Ruby. "It seems ages since I've eaten."

"Well then, tea is the order of the day."

They stopped at a little tea shop. Alfonso ordered a huge plate of scrambled eggs, tea, toast, scones, jam and cream, plus an extra plate of cream cakes.

"Tuck in, my dear girl. There's plenty more where that came from."

Ruby was still uncertain what to make of her newly acquired uncle. He seemed pleasant enough. She knew he had a temper because she had seen how he'd behaved towards Miss Pinkerton, not that she didn't deserve it. The most important thing was that he'd got back the lamp and wand, so he couldn't be all bad, could he?

"You don't look one little bit like my father," she said, feeling braver.

"No, my dear little girl," said Alfonso. "We were as different as chalk and cheese. Alas, your father was the golden boy – I had nothing like his talents. However, I hope I don't over-flatter myself by saying that I am now a magician to be reckoned with."

"I wonder why my father never said anything about you," said Ruby.

"It breaks my heart," said Alfonso, "to remember these sad things, but when your

father and I were little boys, we would
fight, as lads do. I am sorry to say I was
jealous of him. To my everlasting regret, we
fell out and I swore I would never see him
again. So many years have passed; so much
water has flowed under the bridge . . .
When I heard of his tragic end, it broke my
heart, dear girl."

He brought out a large spotted hanky and blew his nose like a trumpet. The little tea shop went quiet, and everyone turned to look.

"You see, dear girl," he said, "they all recognize the Great Alfonso." He had now lost all interest in talking about anything other than himself, a subject he knew a lot about.

It was early in the evening when they arrived in Fizzlewick. Ruby was pleased to see Alfonso lived above a small magic shop. As he parked outside she caught glimpses of all sorts of interesting boxes and books, cloaks and hats in the window.

Above the door a painted sign creaked in the wind. It read:

ALFONSO
SpELS AnD MaJiC

"Excuse me," said Ruby, "why does your sign say –"

"Wonderful, isn't it?" interrupted Alfonso. "I painted it myself. I bought the shop off an old magician friend of mine, after a fortune cookie prophesied 'the door to your future is in a basement.' I like a good riddle, my dear child!"

Ruby was baffled. "Why did you buy this shop if your future lay in a basement?" she asked.

"Well, my friend said the shop had got the better of him," said Alfonso. "There was a door in the basement that wouldn't open. He was convinced there was some great secret behind it. He tried everything to get it open, and in the end he decided to give up and retire to the seaside. When I heard the words 'door' and 'basement', I knew I must buy the shop. One should never underestimate a fortune cookie!" said Alfonso grandly.

"And have you opened the door to the basement?" asked Ruby.

"That's quite enough questions for one day, dear girl," said Alfonso, sounding a little irritable. Ruby didn't dare ask anything else.

And that was how Ruby found herself living in a flat over a magic shop.

11

To begin with everything seemed to go well. It was a lot more exciting than being at Grimlocks. Alfonso was generosity itself. On her first day he took her shopping at the department store of wonders and spells, and made a great show of choosing her a dress.

"You can't wear that school uniform any more, child," said Alfonso. "It clashes with the décor."

Ruby tried on dress after dress until

Alfonso found one he liked, a pink frock with a huge bow.

"Now you look like my niece, dear heart," said Alfonso.

Ruby hadn't liked her school uniform one little bit, but she liked the pink frock even less. She wanted to say so, but Alfonso wasn't listening. He was thinking about what a great actor he was, and how well he played the part of a generous and caring uncle, which of course could not have been further from the truth.

Alfonso had followed the careers of Mr Genie and his wife Myrtle with starstruck envy. He had seen amazing things happen when the lovely Mrs Genie waved her magic wand and watched the audience gasp in wonder as Mr Genie wafted out of his magic lamp. So when he heard of their untimely deaths, he saw his chance. If only he could get his hands on that lamp and that wand, how his life would change! He too would become a great magician. He would be the Great Alfonso.

Alfonso was all prepared to spend his life savings on buying the lamp and the wand when he heard that they had been given to the Genies' only child, Ruby. He didn't even know they had a child! She must have great magical powers – that was why they had kept so quiet about her. But he needed that lamp and wand more than Ruby did . . .

That was why Alfonso decided to pretend to be Ruby's uncle and abduct her from Grimlocks School. It had worked like a dream. Miss Pinkerton, the old cabbage leaf, had believed every word he said. Now he had Ruby, and, far more important, he had the lamp and the wand. Alfonso was not going to waste any more time.

12

Ruby couldn't understand what she had done wrong. Alfonso became like an actor taking off his disguise. Gone was the kind and generous uncle who wanted his niece to look her very best - all gone in a puff of blue smoke. In his place there appeared a frightening, bad-tempered man. Ruby could see quite clearly that this was not her uncle.

"I've had enough of this playacting. It's time for you to earn your keep," said

Alfonso. He took the lamp and the wand out of his safe and placed them carefully on a table. He could hardly contain his excitement.

"Now show me the mysteries of the lamp," he said, rubbing his chubby hands together in glee.

Ruby looked at him, amazed. "I don't know what you mean," she said.

Alfonso laughed. "Oh, very funny! Well, if you like you can start by showing me how the wand performs, and we can move on to the lamp later."

"Honest, I don't know anything about them. They weren't mine, they belonged to my mother and father," said Ruby, rather worried by the glint in Alfonso's eye.

"I know that, you stupid little girl," said Alfonso. "That's why I wanted them. You must know what to do. Otherwise, why would your parents have left them to you?"

"I don't know," said Ruby, her eyes

pricking with tears.

"Oh, very touching. I weep for you, I sympathize. Now, no more fun and games," said Alfonso. He was turning redder and redder.

"I'd like to help, but I'm no good at magic," said Ruby, her legs shaking.

"You are toying with the Great Alfonso. You play with me at your peril! Do you think that I would have invested all this time in you if I thought for one miserable moment that you couldn't make the lamp and the wand work?" said Alfonso furiously. "Well, don't just stand there, give the lamp a rub!"

Ruby rubbed the lamp with all her might, but nothing happened.

"I'm sorry," said Ruby, tears pouring down her face. Alfonso let out a cruel laugh. She tried waving the wand around. Nothing happened, except that Ruby was so frightened that she began to shrink.

Alfonso looked a little surprised, but said, "Now you see what the Great Alfonso can do when his anger is aroused!"

Ruby too was surprised to find quite how much she had shrunk. She was now about as tall as the table. She climbed up on to a chair and tried again. Nothing happened, except that she could see her frightened face shining back at her in the lamp.

Alfonso's face had gone purple. His eyes looked as if they might pop out of his head at any moment.

"This is too much. You're playing with me!" yelled Alfonso, stamping his foot.

"Oh dear," thought Ruby. "I'm shrinking again."

"Do you think that I, the Great Alfonso, would have gone to so much trouble, pretending to be your uncle, squandering money on you, if I had known for one minute what a stupid, useless little worm you would turn out to be . . ."

Here Alfonso stopped and stared at
Ruby. She had shrunk to about twenty
centimetres.

"Now you see the
spells I can cast on
little girls who don't do
what they're told!"
shouted Alfonso.
"You're useless!"

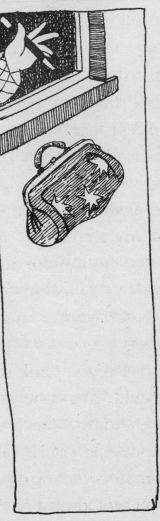

And he picked
Ruby up and threw
her inside an old
handbag that was
lying around. With one
click it snapped shut
and Ruby's world
went dark. "Good
riddance to bad
rubbish!" yelled
Alfonso, and he flung
open the window and
hurled the bag out.

Ruby felt herself flying through the air. She tumbled over something in the dark, hurting her

knee and hitting her head on something hard. Then Ruby knew no more.

Just then a lady who had been buying a trick in the magic shop came out into the street. She was surprised to see a handbag falling out of the sky. With one nifty move she caught it, then looked up to see if someone had dropped it by mistake.

"Is this yours?" she called to Alfonso as he was shutting the window.

"No, madam," said Alfonso. "What would I want with a handbag?"

"Fancy," said Aunt Hat (for that was the

lady's name), "it must be my lucky day. This bag could come in very handy."

Just how handy, she was about to find out.

13

When Ruby woke up, she had no idea how long she had been in the handbag. She had lost all sense of time. All she knew was that she was hungry and frightened. Perhaps she had been forgotten, left on a shelf in Alfonso's magic shop. It would be years before anyone thought to look inside the bag. When they did, they would find a tiny skeleton.

Ruby started to cry. This was really bad.

Worse than being an orphan, worse than Grimlocks, worse than being with Alfonso.

Suddenly the clasp of the bag flew open. Ruby could see daylight and a string of ladies' knickers hanging on a clothesline.

Aunt Hat was in a cheerful mood. Not every day, she thought, do you get given a handbag, even if it does come flying at you through the sky. She got out a duster. "With a little polish," she said to herself, "that bag will look as good as new."

It is hard to know who was more startled when she opened the handbag, Ruby or Aunt Hat. It is true to say both were in for a very big surprise. What Ruby saw was a round, kind face staring down at her. What Aunt Hat saw nearly made her jump out of her skin. It's not every day you find a teeny weeny little girl in a handbag.

Ruby's luck was about to change. Of all the people she could have landed on, she couldn't have chosen better than Aunt Hat.

She lived in a small flat that was full of
odds and ends, colours and flowers.
Everything had been put together in a
higgledy-piggledy way that gave the place a
warm, comfortable feeling. Ruby, for the
first time in a long while, felt safe.

They sat together drinking tea at Aunt Hat's kitchen table. Ruby perched on a dolls' house chair, drinking from a tiny cup and saucer, while Aunt Hat cut her small slices of toast and cake.

Ruby was beginning to feel better already. She told Aunt Hat all about her adventure and how she had come to be in the bag in the first place. Aunt Hat's sunny face clouded over when Ruby came to the bit about Alfonso. She was horrified to find that he had taken her so easily from Grimlocks. What was Miss Pinkerton thinking of, letting Ruby go off with that dreadful old magician? What was the world of magic coming to, that's what she would like to know.

"I don't think I'll ever see my father's lamp or my mother's wand again," said Ruby sadly. "I wish I was good at magic like them. All I can do is read, and that's not much use."

"You can read! Oh petal, that is some magic trick!" said Aunt Hat, really impressed. "That is something I've never been able to do."

"Really?" said Ruby.

"Oh yes, petal, to be able to read is worth more than old lamps and wands," said Aunt Hat. "If I could read properly, I might have been able to find myself another job after the magic left me."

"I don't understand," said Ruby.

Aunt Hat laughed. "I haven't introduced myself properly. I am Aunt Hat, a children's conjurer." She pointed towards a beautiful collection of hats hanging on the wall. "That's how I got my name, on account of the wonderful hats I wore. When I was a

wee bit younger than I am now I was a rather good children's entertainer, but something happened, and I lost my magic touch. These days I'm grateful for any little job that comes my way."

"That's very sad. What are you going to do?" asked Ruby.

"I can only do my best with my fisherman's vest," said Aunt Hat cheerfully. "As it happens I'm booked to do a children's party tomorrow, because Cecil the snake man has been taken ill. But I have a feeling that now I've met you, Ruby Genie, maybe, just maybe, things might get better."

14

That night Ruby slept in Aunt Hat's
bedroom, in a little dolls' house, on a
wrought iron bed with a feather mattress
and feather pillows. Ruby read Aunt Hat
Aladdin for a bedtime story. For the first
time in ages she went to sleep happy.

The next day the sun shone through the
windows and the flat twinkled in the sunny
light. Aunt Hat was busy making tiny
pancakes for breakfast. She had laid a

miniature table with dolls' house plates and cutlery. In the middle of the table was a small bunch of glass flowers.

After breakfast, Aunt Hat found a box of dolls' clothes for Ruby to look through.

"I have boxes and boxes of useless small things, don't ask me why! I just love collecting dolls' house furniture and doll size clothes." Aunt Hat laughed merrily. "I must have known that one day I would meet you."

Ruby had hated the clothes Alfonso had bought for her and made her wear, so she was thrilled to be able to look through Aunt Hat's boxes of delights. She finally chose a hat with bells hanging from it with a tiny spoon sewn on to the front, a pair of baggy trousers and a very beautiful old coat covered in stars. It was almost as if it had been made for her.

"Don't you look wonderful!" said Aunt Hat. "Quite the magician if you don't mind me saying."

That afternoon Ruby went with Aunt Hat
to the children's birthday party. Aunt Hat had
gone to considerable trouble to clean out
the handbag. She had removed the bit of old
orange peel that had been left in there and
now the bag shone inside and out. Ruby sat
on a dolls' house armchair so that she would
be comfortable while travelling. She had a
torch so she could see in the dark and a ladder
so that she could climb up and look out.

The party was held in a very grand house in Canal Street. A rather over-anxious mother greeted Aunt Hat.

"Oh hello," she said. "You haven't come a moment too soon. The little darlings have got through all the games and demolished Pass the Parcel, and now they want entertaining before tea."

Aunt Hat was shown into a sitting room where a stage had been set up. A little girl in a huge pink frilly dress came over. She looked rather like a marshmallow on legs.

"Here is the birthday girl," said the mother in a flustered voice. "Charlotte, say hello to Aunt Hat."

"Oh Mummy," said Charlotte in disgust. "I thought you'd got the snake man. You know, the one Miranda had at her party. She got to hold a tarantula."

"Now precious," said her mother, "you know he isn't well. We were very lucky to get Aunt Hat."

71

Charlotte stamped her foot on the floor.

"I don't want Aunt Hat. She's for babies!"
And Charlotte left the room, slamming the
door behind her. Her mother gave a little
nervous laugh.

"She's just a little over-excited. You
know how it is. They wait all year for this

day and one does so want to get it right."

Aunt Hat was left alone to set up. She opened the bag so that Ruby could see out. In no time at all the room filled up with noisy giggling girls in party dresses.

"I had a sword swallower for my party," said one little girl with a pink bow.

"That's nothing," said a plump girl in blue. "I had a fire eater at mine. He lay on a bed of nails and I got to stand on him. When he got up there were real nail marks all down his back."

Aunt Hat tried to get their attention but nobody seemed in the least bit interested in what she was doing. Ruby had by now climbed up her little ladder so that she could see what was going on. She had to agree that Aunt Hat was pretty terrible.

"I know how you do that," shouted one girl from the front. Charlotte's parents were now in quite a state as the noise of bored children rose to a deafening din.

"I could do better myself," said her father crossly.

"She was all I could get at such short notice," the mother snapped back. The birthday girl burst into tears.

"This is the worst birthday ever," she sobbed.

Her mother turned desperately to Aunt Hat. "Do something, anything, for goodness sake," she wailed.

15

What happened next not only silenced the whole party but took Aunt Hat completely by surprise. Hidden in the handbag, Ruby wanted to help Aunt Hat so badly, she felt she was going to burst. She couldn't bear the idea of all these children not liking Aunt Hat's magic show. She could see tears in Aunt Hat's eyes as the children began to jeer. They shouldn't make fun of such a kind friend! If only she could do something to help - anything - like make lots of sweets appear! She closed her eyes and concentrated. As she did so, she felt a tingle go through her whole body. It was then that Ruby realized two things: first, the room seemed to have gone very quiet, and secondly, and far more amazing, Ruby Genie was doing her first ever magic trick.

The children watched as the first few sweets flew up in the air. They stopped when Aunt Hat put her bag on the table. It's difficult to make sweets appear when you're wobbling about. The children began to shout, "We want more! We want more!" Then a fountain of sweets shot out like fireworks, in all directions and in all different colours.

When the display finished, Aunt Hat was so astonished she couldn't think what to say.

The children clapped and cheered. "More! More!" they shouted again.

Aunt Hat looked in the bag. Inside she saw Ruby Genie with a huge smile on her face, and the beginnings of a birthday cake. Aunt Hat had just enough time to say, "For my grand finale," before the birthday cake came floating out of the bag. Aunt Hat caught it with great aplomb. (That was one

thing Aunt Hat had always been good at, catching things.)

The cake was followed by a shower of blazing candles that formed the words "Happy Birthday" in the air before whizzing down like darts to position themselves in the icing.

"How did you do that?" asked Charlotte.

Aunt Hat laughed. "The secret is in the bag," she said.

After that the party was a great success. At going home time, Charlotte looked a little sheepish as she said to Aunt Hat that it was the best magic show she had ever seen. All her friends wanted Aunt Hat to entertain at their parties. In fact, Charlotte's parents were so pleased with the way things had gone that they had paid Aunt Hat extra.

That night Aunt Hat and Ruby went home in a taxi.

16

The next few weeks were a whirlwind of
children's parties. Ruby was really enjoying
herself. She liked nothing better than being
hidden in the bag. It gave her all the
courage she needed, knowing no one could
see her doing her magic.

At first, she could only make sweets and
cakes appear. Aunt Hat wouldn't have
minded one little bit if she had just stuck to
that, for all the children loved them.

But Aunt Hat had a feeling that sweets were just the beginning. Ruby had worked out that as long as she had a picture of what she wanted in her head, she could usually make it appear. At first floating unformed out of the bag, in no time at all it took on the shape of whatever Ruby was imagining.

The children in the audience knew nothing about Ruby. What they saw was Aunt Hat waving her wand and making the most magical things appear from her bag. Sometimes things appeared even when she wasn't waving her wand. The truth was that Aunt Hat was never quite sure what Ruby would come up with next, whether it would last any length of time or vanish at once in a puff of rainbow smoke.

Every day Ruby's magic was getting stronger and her confidence was growing. There were a few teething problems, like the time she imagined a snake with two hundred legs which made all the children run and hide.

The parents laughed nervously and looked most relieved when it vanished, but Aunt Hat didn't mind a bit. That was what Ruby

loved about Aunt Hat. Whatever she came up with, Aunt Hat would say, when they were safely home, "Well, wasn't that amazing! Aren't you the cleverest magician ever!"

Aunt Hat had had the bright idea of sewing a secret compartment into the bag, where Ruby could hide. The grand finale of every show came when Aunt Hat lifted up the bag so all the children could see that it was quite empty. No one knew about Ruby, and that was the way both of them wanted it to stay.

17

Aunt Hat's magic handbag was becoming the talk of the town. It wasn't only children who wanted to see her magic show. Offers began to pour in from around the world: Paris offered her the Opera House to star in; New York, the Met; London, Covent Garden. All were willing to pay sums of money Aunt Hat had only dreamt of. Aunt Hat was becoming quite a star. Her picture appeared on the front page of the Wizards' World. The headline read: AUNT HAT – THE MOST EXTRAORDINARY MAGICIAN EVER! OR IS THE SECRET IN THE BAG?

Everyone wanted to know how the magic was done, and more to the point, how had such a hopeless magician as Aunt Hat become an overnight sensation?

But things were getting a little out of control. It was like winning the Lottery, only better and a bit more worrying.

Aunt Hat was right to worry that with all this attention, sooner or later, she would come to the notice of a certain somebody, and it wouldn't take this certain somebody long to work out the secret of the magic bag. When that happened, Aunt Hat knew that Ruby would be in great danger.

Ruby was blissfully unaware of Aunt Hat's worries or the razzamatazz that was surrounding them. She was enjoying being with Aunt Hat and finding out about the fun in magic. She had never felt happier. She had even stopped worrying about whether the magic was due to her or the bag. Aunt Hat was right, it didn't matter.

But now they had been asked to perform in such grand theatres Ruby felt the time had come to see if she could fly. After all, her father and mother both could. She had been practising for the past week. It was lucky that Aunt Hat was so good at catching, otherwise Ruby might really have come to grief.

She was forever launching herself off the ends of tables, convinced that this time she would defy gravity and fly, but she had no

success. She must be doing something wrong. Her father had been able to waft out of his lamp like a true genie should, as well as walking on two legs like everybody else. Her mother had also been good at flying, though she never did it in polite society. Flying, she used to say, is so theatrical and looks out of place in a sitting room. Ruby wondered whether, if she still had her father's lamp, she would be able to waft or if she had her mother's wand would she be able to fly?

It wasn't long before the Great Alfonso saw the pictures of Aunt Hat and her famous bag. At first he took little notice. The rumours he had heard about Aunt Hat were too far-fetched to be believed. He knew for a fact that Aunt Hat was useless at magic. There must be some mistake, of that he was sure. Why, the other day, she had been spotted talking to this bag!

"As mad as a hairbrush," Alfonso had chuckled to himself. That was before he'd

seen the pictures in the newspaper.

Alfonso's chuckle turned to rage. Why that was his bag, if he was not mistaken, and that must be Ruby Genie doing the magic. How dare that good-for-nothing little twerp treat him, the Great Alfonso, so badly! He would get her back and this time Ruby would do as she was told. She would make that lamp work if it was the last thing she ever did.

18

Miss Pinkerton was in one of her rare good moods. The Grand Wizard had said he wanted to make another visit to the school. It seemed that he had been most impressed last time he was there. Miss Pinkerton was positively purring with delight. Thank goodness, she thought to herself, that I got rid of that troublesome Ruby Genie. What on earth possessed me to give that child a scholarship? Miss Fisher was right, it was

probably the reading that had ruined her.
But now all that was safely behind them.
The main thing was that the Grand Wizard
was clearly pleased with the talent
displayed by the pupils and staff of
Grimlocks. Congratulations were in order, of
that she was sure.

But, oh dear me, poor Miss Pinkerton
was in for a nasty shock.

The Grand Wizard looked as though he
would explode with rage when Miss
Pinkerton, in a cheerful voice, told him that
Ruby Genie was no longer at the school. He
looked so cross, in fact, that for one moment
Miss Pinkerton feared she would be turned
into a toad.

"You have done what?" he shouted. "I thought you were looking after her! Instead, you let her go off with a man you have never set eyes on before, who claims to be her uncle! What on earth possessed you?"

Miss Pinkerton was taken aback. "He seemed a very nice man, I thought. Ruby is a lucky girl to have such a caring uncle."

"Miss Pinkerton," said the Grand Wizard slowly, trying to contain his anger. "Am I hearing you right? You let a ten-year-old orphan go off with a complete stranger because he told you he was her uncle and he seemed a nice man?"

Miss Pinkerton looked worried. "I thought it was for the best, her being so bad at magic and always having her nose stuck in a book."

She had hardly finished speaking when the Grand Wizard let out a growl. "You thought, did you! The stars save us from any more of your ghastly thoughts. Did he take the lamp and the wand too?"

"Yes," admitted Miss Pinkerton a little sheepishly. "Though I did try to suggest that he kept them in return for her school fees."

The Grand Wizard raised his bushy eyebrows in disbelief. "Oh really! Do I make myself clear when I tell you that Ruby has no uncles? He wanted Ruby because he saw something you have woefully failed to see – that Ruby is destined to become one of the great genies of our times."

"But Grand Wizard," said Miss Pinkerton feebly, "when you came to our Open Day you seemed rather put out with Ruby."

The Grand Wizard said very slowly, as if talking to a three-year-old, "On the contrary, Miss Pinkerton. I was amazed to see her there. I came today to see how you were managing. But what do I find? No Ruby!"

Miss Pinkerton was lost for words. "Are you sure," she said, trying to look on the bright side, "that we are talking about the same girl? I mean, you don't think you're muddling her up with her friend, Lily?"

"No, Miss Pinkerton," said the Grand Wizard, "I have not muddled her up with anyone. Ruby Genie was the girl I saw trying, if I remember correctly, to pull a rabbit from a hat."

"Yes," said Miss Pinkerton, puffing herself up, "and failing."

"Yes, failing to pull a miserable rabbit from a hat, but doing something far more extraordinary – shrinking in size."

Miss Pinkerton turned white and sat down heavily on a chair.

"Oh dear, I didn't think anything of it, I mean it wasn't the first time . . ." Her voice trailed off, as all the clocks began to chime the hour. The Grand Wizard frowned and raised his hand. The room was silent.

"Quite," said the Grand Wizard. "Not even her vain and silly parents had seen what a wonderful little genie she would turn out to be. I was impressed that you had spotted a very gifted child. Even Wizodean Academy had failed to see her talent. I thought I had underestimated you as a headmistress. I was delighted that you had given her a scholarship. And when you assured me she was in good hands, I was doubly pleased."

"Oh dear me," whimpered Miss Pinkerton. "What have I done?"

"What indeed," said the Grand Wizard. "Do you have any idea how powerful that lamp is? Once its power is started Ruby could be caught in it forever. Due to your woeful stupidity, Ruby Genie is now in great danger."

19

The plan was so simple that it made the Great Alfonso smile. It would be like stealing candy from a baby.

Aunt Hat had just finished performing her magic show at a house in Market Street. As usual a crowd of people were waiting for autographs. It was then that Alfonso made his move.

"Madam, that is my handbag," he said loudly.

Aunt Hat took no notice. Alfonso wasn't the least put out.

"Lady, I was talking to you. That is my bag. You stole it from me."

The crowd let out a gasp. Aunt Hat looked flustered.

"I want my bag back," said Alfonso, and he grabbed hold of the bag and to Aunt Hat's astonishment began to walk away with it, as cool as a cucumber.

"Come back!" she yelled. "You have no right to take my bag!"

The crowd ran after Alfonso and a large man got the bag off him and handed it to Aunt Hat.

"Oh thank you," said Aunt Hat, much relieved. Alfonso glared at her.

"I, the Great Alfonso, accuse you of being nothing more than a common thief," he said.

"That's absurd!" said Aunt Hat.

"Now look here, my good man, that's no way to talk to a lady," said a gentleman in the crowd.

"Quite right," said another.

"Well!" said the large man who had rescued the bag from Alfonso. "There is a simple way to solve this problem. The magistrate can sort it out."

The magistrate was rather surprised to see her courtroom fill up with so many people. She was even more surprised by Alfonso's claims that this famous handbag had once belonged to him.

"You have accused Miss Hat of stealing this handbag. Would you please tell the court how it came to be stolen in the first place."

"With pleasure," said Alfonso. Here he was, the Great Alfonso, centre stage, with everyone looking at him. What bliss!

"That woman," he said in a theatrical voice, "took my bag from me, just after I'd finished doing a special piece of magic, which involved creating a genie to put inside it." He paused and sighed. "I was, as you can imagine, exhausted after my exertions. I put the bag on the windowsill. Unfortunately a gust of wind blew it off, and it fell onto the street below. It was caught by that woman there. I asked, nay, I begged her to give it back but she ran off with it down the street. I tried to run after her but by the time I got downstairs to the street she was gone." Alfonso blew his nose loudly and dabbed his eyes. "That woman has robbed the Great Alfonso of his fortune and his fame. I assure you that without my magic, that bag is worthless."

There was silence in the court. "This is a very serious accusation," said the magistrate

to Aunt Hat. "How do you defend yourself?"

Aunt Hat stood up. "I didn't steal the bag. I would never do such a thing. It is true that the bag was thrown from Alfonso's window and that I caught it. I asked him if it is was his and he said 'No, what would I want with a handbag?' Those were his very words. I took it home and the rest is history."

"The true owner of the bag will know what it contains," said the magistrate. "Mr Alfonso, please tell the court what was in the bag."

"Nothing," said Alfonso grandly. "Only a small genie and all my hopes and dreams."

The magistrate looked in the bag. She could see nothing. She put her hand in the bag. She could feel nothing. She turned the bag upside down. No genie. Ruby was well hidden.

"The bag may well contain all your hopes and dreams, Mr Alfonso, but it has no genie in it," said the magistrate. "As far as I can see, it is completely empty. Miss Hat, would you like to tell the court what you had in the bag?"

"Oh, nothing much," said Aunt Hat. "A hanky, a purse, a hat and of course a hatstand, a table and chair, a teapot, cups and saucers, and don't forget the plate of cakes. Did I mention the candlesticks? Then

of course there's my umbrella - one is never sure what the weather will do. And oh dear, I nearly forgot the pond and the ducks. I can't go anywhere without them."

"This is ridiculous. This woman is making fun of the law," said Alfonso.

The magistrate opened the bag for the

second time. "There is, as I said, nothing in this bag."

"There must be some mistake," said Aunt Hat. "I know for a fact that I put those things in this morning. Well, wait a moment. I might have left my purse at home after all. I do hope not."

All this time, Ruby had been hiding in her secret compartment, trying not to be seen or felt. She had been quite joggled about when the magistrate had tipped the bag upside down.

The magistrate was about to give her verdict when, to her astonishment, a purse came flying out of the bag.

"Oh good," said Aunt Hat. "I thought I hadn't left it at home."

The courtroom soon filled up with a hatstand, a table laid for tea, a plate of cakes, three candlesticks, a pond complete with ducks and weed, and last of all, a large hanky that flew straight into Aunt Hat's pocket. A loud cheer went up for Aunt Hat.

The case was about to be dismissed when Miss Pinkerton came charging in.

"Arrest that man!" she shouted at the top of her voice, pointing at Alfonso. Then she marched into the duckpond.

The magistrate looked taken aback. "Order in the court!" she said. "Order!"

Miss Pinkerton, her mouth full of duckweed, cried out again, "Arrest that man! He has abducted a child!"

In the chaos that followed, the Great Alfonso disappeared and so did Aunt Hat's bag.

20

Aunt Hat had never felt so miserable. She had lost Ruby, the one little person she loved. What was she going to do? And, more important, how was she going to get Ruby back? She would have to work out a plan. Alfonso must be stopped before he did anything dreadful.

"No time for tea. It's time for action," said Aunt Hat to an empty kitchen.

"That's a pity," came back a small voice.

"I was feeling quite hungry."

Aunt Hat couldn't believe her eyes. There, standing on the kitchen table, was Ruby. "Oh my petal, it's you, it really is you! How did you do it?"

"Well," said Ruby, feeling rather pleased with herself, "I flew. I was so scared of being taken away by Alfonso, I just hid under the hanky, and concentrated very hard, hoping it would work, and thank goodness, it did!"

Never had two people been more pleased to see each other. They sat drinking tea and eating chocolate cake and talking about what to do next.

"Why do you think Miss Pinkerton turned up?" said Ruby.

"I suppose," said Aunt Hat, "because she felt guilty at having let you go off with Alfonso in the first place."

"Silly old Miss Pinkerton," laughed Ruby. "It served her right when she fell into the duckpond, with the weeds and the ducks all flapping about."

"I had no idea that pond was so deep," said Aunt Hat. "Now, down to serious business. What are we going to do about Alfonso? As soon as he realizes you aren't inside the bag, he's going to come looking for you."

"Why?" asked Ruby. "I can't make the lamp work, or the wand either. I don't know how."

"I don't think the lamp and the wand matter any more," said Aunt Hat. "He just wants you, because you're so amazing at magic."

Ruby looked worried. "I don't think it's anything to do with me. I think the magic is in the bag."

"Let's find out," said Aunt Hat. "See if you can make some sweets appear without the bag, my petal."

Ruby tried her hardest, but nothing

happened. "It's no good," she said, looking very small and sad.

"Well, this will never do. What right has that old buffoon to go around taking things that aren't his?" said Aunt Hat, putting on her hat and coat. "We'll just have to go to his flat and get the bag back, and while we're about it we'll get the lamp and the wand too."

That evening, under the cover of darkness, they set out for Alfonso's magic shop. Ruby travelled in Aunt Hat's pocket. Fortunately no one was around to see them break in.

The shop was scary, full of jars filled with sinister-looking things and masks that looked like real faces in the darkness. Aunt Hat tripped over something and it made a loud noise, like a clap of thunder.

"Oh pants!" she whispered. "We're in for it now!"

They waited, half expecting the lights to

go on and Alfonso to be standing there, but all was quiet.

"He keeps the lamp and the wand upstairs in a safe," said Ruby. Aunt Hat shone a torch to light the way.

Alfonso's room looked as if a hurricane had struck it. He had obviously had one of his famous tantrums. Everything in it had been broken or smashed. Aunt Hat picked up the bag. It was quite battered and turned inside out. Then she tripped over the lamp which had been thrown carelessly on the floor. Aunt Hat put Ruby and the lamp on the one remaining table for safekeeping, and started looking for the wand.

"What a touching scene!" Alfonso's voice boomed in the quiet room. Aunt Hat nearly jumped out of her skin and dropped the torch. Alfonso turned the lights on.

"Don't move," he said. "I've got you both now." He made a grab for Ruby. "Well, isn't this Alfonso's lucky day?"

"Oh pants," said Aunt Hat as Alfonso tied her up.

"I can now add housebreaking to your

list of crimes," Alfonso chuckled. "As for you," he said to Ruby, "we have work to do. This time there is no playing with the Great Alfonso."

Just then there was a loud banging at the door. "Oh ramblasting!" said Alfonso. "I will not be disturbed!"

Holding Ruby tightly in one sweaty hand, and the lamp in the other, he climbed down the stairs to the basement. Ruby felt very frightened. Alfonso's footsteps echoed as if the basement went on for ever. She could hear lapping water not that far away. Was he going to drown her?

Alfonso put Ruby on a workbench with the lamp next to her.

"Now my dear little genie girl, make that lamp work."

Ruby closed her eyes and tried her best, but nothing happened.

"It will be the end of you, you miserable child, if you don't," yelled Alfonso.

"I can't do magic without my bag," said Ruby bravely, though her teeth were chattering.

Alfonso grabbed her and rushed upstairs again, holding her tightly. The banging on the door was getting louder. There was not a minute to lose.

He picked up the bag.

"I can't do it without Aunt Hat either," said Ruby.

Alfonso didn't say a word. He untied Aunt Hat and took her back down to the basement. Now voices could be heard shouting, "Open up in the name of the law!"

Alfonso bolted the door so that no one could come in.

"I have, as always, been generosity itself," said Alfonso. "I have even let you have this ridiculous old cabbage leaf to help you. Now Ruby, for the last time, make that lamp work!"

Ruby couldn't. What she could do was

make the lamp fly, but Alfonso was too quick for her. He grabbed the bag and in his rage threw it at the cellar door.

As he did so the door began to glow. On it appeared the words:

The Land of Wonders Enter at Your Peril

"What does it say?" shouted Alfonso, pointing at the letters.

"Enter at your peril," said Ruby faintly.

And as she spoke, the door swung open and a bright golden light shone out. There before them was an orchard of glass trees, hung with precious stones and sparkling like rainbows.

"I'm rich!" cried Alfonso. "Richer than all the kings in the world!" He stumbled towards the door like a drunken man.

Suddenly there was a wail, as if from the centre of the earth, and a voice as sad as sorrow said, "You have no right to enter here."

"Yes I have," said Alfonso. "A fortune cookie told me the door to my future lay in the basement."

The door slammed shut.

"No, no!" shouted Alfonso, stamping his foot. He turned to Ruby. "Open it again! I order you to!"

" She doesn't know how," said Aunt Hat.

"Oh be quiet, you old cabbage leaf," said Alfonso.

The door began to glow again. More words appeared, this time in silver. To her surprise, Ruby read:

Come in Ruby Genie Welcome

Ruby's fears vanished and all at once the door began to shrink down to her size. She turned the handle and the door opened to reveal the same orchard, but now all on a tiny scale.

"Get a move on, girl! There's no time to lose," said Alfonso. "If you're not back in five minutes with all the jewels you can carry, your precious Aunt Hat is in trouble."

Ruby walked though the door. A river of gold ran through the orchard and silver blossom fell in a cool breeze. Jewels of red, blue, green and purple tinkled down from the trees. Ruby picked up as many as she could carry and put them in her pockets.

She was just about to leave when she saw a beautiful little flower like a daisy, all made out of precious stones. She bent down and picked it up to give it to Aunt Hat, and as she did so a voice as sweet as happiness spoke to her.

"Ruby," said the voice, "all the magic you need is in you. You are loved."

22

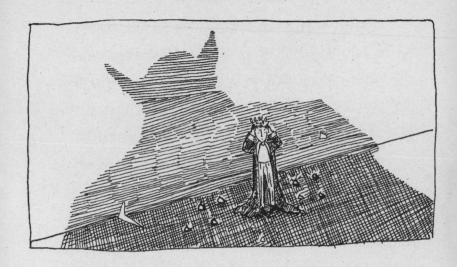

"Give me the stones!" screamed Alfonso. "Stop playing about and give them to me!"

Ruby emptied her pockets and put all the tiny little stones on the workbench.

"That's it?" said Alfonso. "Is that all you could bring the Great Alfonso?"

He was interrupted by four policemen who came charging into the basement followed by Miss Pinkerton.

"Arrest that man!" ordered Miss

Pinkerton. "He is responsible for the murder of Ruby Genie!"

"I think that's a little far-fetched," said Aunt Hat mildly. "Ruby is over there," and she pointed to Ruby, who was standing on the workbench. Miss Pinkerton let out a piercing scream, as if she'd been stabbed.

"What have you done to her? She's so small!"

The policemen thought Miss Pinkerton had been wounded, and rushed to rescue her. In the confusion, Alfonso grabbed Ruby and popped her into her father's lamp. He held it up as if he was about to throw it.

"Out of my way," he shouted, "or the little girl gets it!"

Nobody could have known what would happen next.

23

Ruby felt her body becoming silver and liquid. A tingle rushed through her and she felt that she had turned to air. To her amazement she began to waft out of the lamp, and to the horror of everyone there she said in a voice that didn't sound like her own, "I am the genie of the lamp."

Alfonso let out a terrible laugh and did a little jig.

"I want you to tie up all those nasty

people, my dear genie. Then bring me all the larger stones!"

Aunt Hat looked on, stunned, as Ruby Genie began to grow. She got bigger and bigger until she filled the entire basement.

"The Great Alfonso commands the genie of the lamp!" said Alfonso in a grand voice. This was the moment he had been waiting for all his life. Now nothing could stop him becoming one of the most powerful magicians ever. He turned to Aunt Hat, Miss Pinkerton and the four policemen and said, "Now you see what the Great Alfonso can do when his anger is aroused!"

Ruby didn't seem to be paying attention to Alfonso's words. She just hovered.

"Go on, do as I say!" ordered Alfonso, although he looked a little worried. This was not how things should be.

At that moment there was a sound like waves crashing on a stony beach. As if from nowhere the Grand Wizard appeared.

"Leave the lamp immediately, Ruby," said the Grand Wizard in a loud clear voice, "and get back inside the bag. If you do not you will be the slave of that lamp for ever."

"Mind your own business, you muddling old fool. This is my genie and there's nothing you can do about it," sneered Alfonso.

"Oh, isn't there?" said the Grand Wizard, who had had quite enough of Alfonso. He raised his hand and immediately Alfonso was frozen like a statue.

Ruby was still hovering half in and half out of the lamp.

"I don't think Ruby can get out," said Aunt Hat anxiously.

"What I need is the wand, and quickly," said the Grand Wizard. "Time is running out."

Aunt Hat pushed past the policemen and rushed upstairs. Alfonso's flat was such a mess she didn't know where to look.

Suddenly she saw something twinkling under a chair - the wand! She picked it up and ran back down to the basement. She was only just in time. Ruby was about to be sucked back into the lamp.

The Grand Wizard touched the lamp with the wand. There was a flash of lightning and the lamp shattered into a thousand pieces.

"Oh!" cried Aunt Hat. "What's happened to Ruby?"

"Try the bag," said the Grand Wizard.

Aunt Hat ran over to the bag. There, to her great relief, was Ruby, dazed, as small as ever, but all in one piece. Beside her lay a tiny flower. It was the most beautiful thing Aunt Hat had ever seen.

"It's for you," said Ruby with a smile.

They both looked at the magic door. On it shimmered the words:

Goodbye, Ruby Genie! Your Troubles Are Now Over

"What an extraordinary business," said Aunt Hat. "And what a good thing that you can read, Ruby. Poor Alfonso didn't stand a chance."

24

Things worked out very well. Alfonso was stripped of all his magical powers, which weren't as many as he liked to think. He now works in a sweetshop, having to be nice to children, which he hates.

Miss Pinkerton has given up teaching children. Instead, she runs obedience classes for dogs.

Madame Vanish vanished. Miss Fisher was sent to count peas in a frozen pea factory. Mr Gaspard started a new life doing firework displays, which he was very good at.

The Grand Wizard was so impressed with the way Aunt Hat kept her wits about her that he could think of no one better to be headmistress of Grimlocks School. Aunt Hat wasn't sure if she would be any good at it, but the Grand Wizard was a wise man and he saw that Aunt Hat had a magical gift for bringing out the best in children.

He was right. Aunt Hat was a wonderful teacher and all her pupils did well. Ruby helped her learn to read and Aunt Hat made sure that all the children could read and write as well as do spells. Grimlocks was voted top of the league of all the schools of magic. Much more to the point, all the children were happy.

Ruby's friends were so pleased to see her again. Even if she was tiny, she was still great fun to be with. And here is the most surprising part. Ruby had always thought it was Alfonso's magic that made her tiny, though Aunt Hat had never believed the old windbag had that much magic in him. She, like Zack, was sure that Ruby had shrunk because she was so frightened, and this proved to be right. After only one term back with her schoolfriends, Ruby started to grow again, and in no time at all she was back to her old size.

Aunt Hat made sure that Ruby was kept out of harm's way, and the Grand Wizard put a protective spell on the school so that Ruby's magic was given space to grow.

Aunt Hat and Ruby spend the school holidays together, travelling. Ruby learnt how to use a magic carpet, which meant they were able to fly off on wonderful adventures before term started.

As for the little jewelled flower, Aunt Hat put it in a glass box with some words written underneath:

All the Magic You Need

is in You.

You are Loved.

Lest Ruby should ever forget.

The Strongest Girl in the World

Josie Jenkins, aged eight and three quarters, is good at doing tricks, but she amazes herself and everyone else with her strength when she lifts a table, a car, and even a bus with no effort at all. Mr Two Suit promises to bring her fame and fortune – and so he does. But when Josie and her mum and dad and brother Louis are flown to New York and she becomes a celebrity, she finds that she has to cope with all kinds of ups and downs.

The Boy Who Could Fly

One day the Fat Fairy turns up at Thomas Top's house to grant him a birthday wish. Thomas can't think what to ask for, so he wishes he could fly. That's how Thomas goes from being just an ordinary boy whom no one notices to being the most popular boy in the school. But it makes him sad that grown-ups can't see the amazing things he can do – especially his dad.

The Invisible Boy

Sam's parents have got lost on a trip to the moon and he has been left in the care of the horrible Hilda Hardbottom. Everything seems hopeless. But one night he notices a tiny spaceship in the cabbage patch. Out of it steps a little alien called Splodge. Splodge is a great new friend for him – especially since he knows how to make Sam invisible.

How Sam uses his invisibility to scare the pants off Hilda Hardbottom, and how he finds that being braver makes better, is a wonderful story and a very funny one.